llama llama
home with mama

P9-DCN-598

llama llama home with mama

Anna Dewdney

SCHOLASTIC INC.

Llama Llama, morning light.
Feeling yucky, just not right.

Down to breakfast.
Tiny sneeze.

Sniffle, snuffle.
Tissues, please!

Llama's head
is feeling hot.

Llama's throat
is hurting **lots.**

Achy, fever, stuffy head . . .
Llama Llama, back to bed.

Time to rest.
No school today.

Mama Llama
brings a tray.

Fruity medicine tastes **yucky!**
Llama Llama's throat feels gucky.

Look around. Not much to do.
Trucks are boring. Tractors, too.

Make a tunnel for a train?

Llama Llama, fuzzy brain.

Mama Llama gets a book.
Have a listen.
Take a look.

Heavy eyelids. Drippy nose.
Llama Llama starts to **doze.**

Up again and feeling better.

Draw some pictures.
Make some letters.

Llama wants a sandwich, please!
Mama Llama starts to sneeze.

Lunch is over. Time for toys!
Mama's head does not like noise.

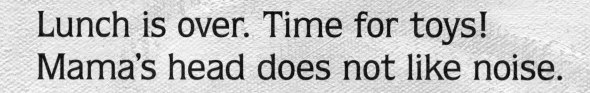

Mama makes a
big **ah-choo!**

Llama's out
of things to do.

Uh oh! Mama's throat is sore.

Being sick is such a **bore.**

Mama coughs,

and Llama yawns. . . .

How long can this day go on?

Mama shnortles, hacks, and wheezes.

Llama Llama's
sick of sneezes!

Soggy tissues,
gobs of guck.
**Sniffing,
snorting,**

Llama Llama, red pajama,
sick and bored, at home with Mama.

WAIT! Llama Llama knows what's best.

Mama Llama
needs a **rest!**

Get more tissues.

Bring a cup.

Fluff a comfy pillow up.

What else could Mama Llama need?

How about some **books** to read?

Just the thing for Llama Llama,
sick at home . . .

but with his mama.

For Ledlie and Leighton,
who love to stay home with their mama

No part of this publication may be reproduced, stored in a retrieval system,
or transmitted in any form or by any means, electronic, mechanical, photocopying,
recording, or otherwise, without written permission of the publisher. For information
regarding permission, write to Viking, a division of Penguin Young Readers Group,
a member of Penguin Group (USA) Inc., 345 Hudson Street, New York, NY 10014.

ISBN 978-0-545-62706-1

Copyright © 2011 by Anna Dewdney. All rights reserved.
Published by Scholastic Inc., 557 Broadway, New York, NY 10012,
by arrangement with Viking, a division of Penguin Young Readers Group,
a member of Penguin Group (USA) Inc. SCHOLASTIC and associated logos
are trademarks and/or registered trademarks of Scholastic Inc.

12 11 10 9 8 7 6 5 4 3 2   13 14 15 16 17 18/0

Printed in the U.S.A.   08

This edition first printing, September 2013

Set in ITC Quorum